USING CR◠

Using Crochet Motifs

Dorothy Standing

Mills & Boon Limited, London

First published in Great Britain 1973 by
Mills & Boon Limited, 17–19 Foley Street, London, WIA IDR

ISBN 0 263.05366.0

Printed Photolitho in Great Britain by
Ebenezer Baylis & Son, Limited
The Trinity Press, Worcester, and London

To Gillie, gratefully

Contents

Introduction

In crochet, a motif is a complete piece of work in geometric shape which can be of any size from something an inch across to unlimited proportions. Seventy years ago they were used for dress trimmings, for doilies and table centres, often intricate in design and each one involving many hours of close work. Today we have a different approach. Fashion demands bold, gay clothes and houses must have bright colourful furnishings. Time spent is an important factor, too, and in modern form motifs are quickly made, while the variety of cottons, wools and other yarns we have to choose from contribute to a compulsive and fascinating hobby. Patterns and shapes are so numerous that they can be adapted to many purposes, from blankets made from oddments to clothes, bags and cushions in planned colour schemes—there's no limit to their application.

Motifs demand a certain amount of expertise in the craft of crochet: one must have absorbed the rules for working 'straight' before attempting shapes such as these, though some of the easier patterns, for example the motif used in the 'cover-up' garment for a child (page 69) or the slipper motif (page 73), would be suitable for a learner to do. Working in one colour, as these are, without the fuss of changing at every round makes for simplicity and speed.

This is a collection of various shapes and sizes with suggestions for their use. You will, I hope, have more ideas for using them, which is all to the good, every pattern having many possibilities. A completely different effect is produced by substituting some other medium than that suggested; by using thicker or finer yarn and hook, by extending the size or reducing it, by converting the motifs to your own needs and ideas. Take any one of them and make a cushion, a long evening skirt, a child's waistcoat. Use paper patterns as a

guide, making the motifs to fit. Work in glitter yarn to make
an evening stole or hand-bag, or at the other extreme use
dish cloth cotton for a set of luncheon or dinner mats for
which almost any of the patterns could be used with added
borders or fringes.

You might even like to make a doily!

It is hoped that the book will be a spur to the imagination and
most of all, a means of encouraging individual expression.

Making Motifs

Here are some points to remember:

1   For long-term items, e.g. blankets and rugs, use materials of one kind, all synthetic or all wool. Synthetic yarns can eventually cut through wool if used together.

2   But interesting effects can be obtained in short-term articles, e.g. bags, belts and clothes which nowadays are worn only while fashion lasts, by introducing varied yarns such as mohair, angora, bouclé and lurex mixtures.

3   Keep texture even. If necessary use two strands of fine yarn together to retain approximate thickness of other wools used.

4   Work over and eliminate ends as you go. This saves 'sewing-in' time eventually, especially on large articles.

5   If motifs are to be sewn together, leave an end on each one for this purpose.

6   When changing colours, start at a different position from where you finished. It should be impossible to discern the beginning of a new round.

7   To join on a new colour at the beginning of a round, draw a loop through the first stitch, leaving a short end and the long end. Now, using the short end, draw a loop through the loop on the hook and pull the two ends tightly. Then make the requisite number of chain (e.g. 3 ch for 1 treble stitch) and continue in pattern, working in pattern, over the short end.

Joining Motifs

1   SLIP STITCH OR DOUBLE CROCHET JOIN

Articles which get hard wear, blankets etc., should be joined
with either of these stitches. This can be done effectively on
the right side using a main colour.

2   SEWING TOGETHER

With tapestry needle, using end left after finishing, sew
through both top threads on edges of motifs, on wrong side.

3   OVER-SEWING THROUGH BACK THREADS ONLY

Sew on wrong side. This leaves a decorative ridge round
each motif on right side.

4   JOINING TOGETHER DURING COURSE OF WORK

Complete one motif, then when working the final side of the
next, make 1 chain at the corner, insert hook into corner of
first motif, draw through a loop and work 1 slip stitch in
second. Repeat at centre and other end. Vary number of
joins with size of motifs.

5   Do not tighten work when joining.

Pressing

This should be approached warily. Crochet's charm is in its
raised stitches which can be spoiled by it.

1   Don't ever try to flatten the fabric.

2   Don't press a fabric if it has clusters or groups in the
pattern.

3   Don't press synthetic yarns or they will lose their spring,
never to return.

4   Do avoid pressing motifs until they are joined together,
when a very light pressure of the iron over a wet cloth will
settle the seams.

Abbreviations...

ch	chain
dc	double crochet
htr	half treble
tr	treble
dtr	double treble
ss	slip stitch
st	stitch
inc	increase
dec	decrease
rep	repeat
*	repeat from this mark
sp	space
ch sp	chain space
tr gr	treble group
gr	group
woh	wool over hook
yoh	yarn over hook

and some stitches

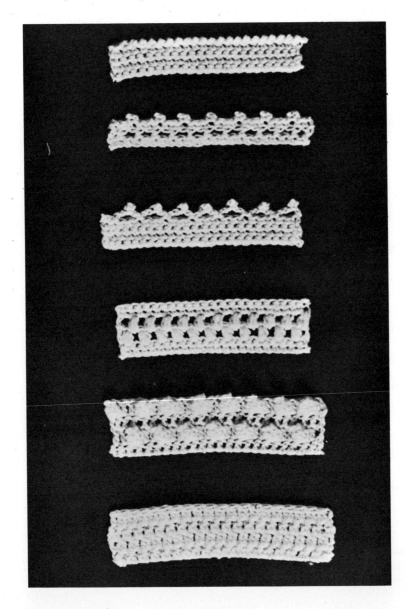

Corded Edge

A useful, decorative edging for any purpose.

Work on right side from left to right instead of from right to left.

Dc backwards, always inserting hook under both horizontal threads.

Picot Edges

1 Ss into 3 sts, 3 ch, ss into same st, repeat. Or dc may be used instead of ss, and with 5 ch, for thicker yarn.

2 Ss into first st, * 5 ch, ss into third ch from hook, 2 ch, miss 2 sts, ss into next. Rep from *.

Puff Stitch

Woh, insert hook and draw through a loop, rep twice (or more) in same st, stretching the loops evenly, woh, draw through all loops, 1 ch. Miss 1 st, rep. A second row is worked in between puff stitches of previous row.

Bobble Stitch

Work 5 tr into the same st, then take hook out of work, insert it in the top of first tr, draw loop of last tr through it, complete with 1 ch.

This stitch also makes an attractive edging.

Group-treble Stitch

Yoh, insert hook in st, draw through a loop (3 loops on hook), yoh, draw through 2 loops, yoh, insert hook into same st, draw through a loop (4 loops on hook), yoh, draw through 2 loops, yoh, draw through 3 loops. Stitch completed.

Comparison chart of hook numbers

I have used the new international hook numbers in the book, but for those who still use the old hook numbers, here is a comparison chart.

New range international	Present range 'wool'
2	14
2·5	12/13
3	11/10
3·5	9
4	8
4·5	7
5	6
5·5	5
6	4
7	2

Buying in grammes

Continental yarns, marked in grammes, are appearing in our shops and British manufacturers are gradually making the change from ounces to grammes. Because of the proposed change to the metric system of weights and measures the following table will be useful when buying materials:

1 oz = 25 gr + 3·35 gr
For 3 ozs buy 4 balls of 25 gr (or 2 balls of 50 gr)
For 7 ozs buy 8 balls of 25 gr
For 12 ozs buy 14 balls of 25 gr
For 16 ozs buy 18 balls of 25 gr
For 20 ozs buy 25 balls of 25 gr

By way of a foreword

From a Learner's Note-book

LESSON 1

'She' assures us that crochet is a pleasant and easy craft,
quick to do, unenergetic and even soothing. We observe the
experts at the other side of the room, churning it out in
great chunks—even *chatting* as they do it. How *can* they?
We hold the hook like a pen and are helped to arrange the
wool over the left hand. Seems awkward but it's said to be
correct. The basic chain. Do twenty-four. It ought to be easy
yet mine somehow turns out to have a surprising variety of
shapes. Keep hoping! Now for the 'simple' stitch, double
crochet. Not so simple and instead of a straight row of
stitches I've a series of mountains and valleys. And it curves
out like a frill. ('Chain was too tight—take it out and start
again.') A little better this time.

Half trebles now and terrifying trebles. Such a struggle and
it looks awful. Did she say 'soothing'?

Homework   Repeat all we have done, eight rows of each
stitch—and remember instructions about TURNING AT
THE ENDS OF ROWS! Can I?

LESSON 2

Homework fair, but stitches have decreased in number and
sampler tends to taper to a point instead of being a nice
rectangle.
(I'm not the only one, thank goodness.)
Variations on the basics this week. It begins to look quite
pretty, if only the edges would keep straight. But the wool
actually *stays* round the little finger of the left hand and the
hook has stopped wobbling like a divining rod.

Homework   Another sampler (we'll have kettle-holders for all time!)

Must try harder.

LESSON 3

I did, and am wearing an invisible halo. A little praise goes a long way. Working in rounds this week, but only in double crochet—which really *is* simple, I find! This is interesting. Increasing—second stitch into back of stitch only so as not to make a big hole. Must remember that. Round we go—it's beginning to look like a beret. Now some decreasing—two stitches joined into one ('Don't hop over one!')—that's easy.
Decrease every other round now. It really *is* a little beret! Might fit Rosemary's baby doll. Exciting. Have actually made something.

Homework   A full-sized beret from teacher's pattern.

LESSON 4

Homework fairly O.K. and almost wearable.

Starting MOTIFS this week. Now we're really getting somewhere.

Might even get a hot-water bottle for homework!

I'm enjoying this now. It's almost all the things she said it was.

Off we go . . . 6 ch in a ring and join . . .

ROUNDS

Two flower motifs

These can be sewn on to children's T-shirts or as a decoration on toddlers' tunics. They are made in 4-ply wool (hook 3·50), but any may be used.

One-Colour Motif

3½″ (9 cm) diameter

6 ch in a ring.

Row 1: 3 ch (= 1 tr). * 2 ch, 1 tr in ring. Rep from *. End with ss in top of 3 ch. (8 ch sps.)

Row 2: Into each ch sp work 1 dc, 2 ch, 2 tr, 2 ch, 1 dc. End with 1 ss in first of 2 ch.

Row 3: 1 dc in each of the two trs, 4 ch. Rep. Join with ss in first dc.

Row 4: 3 ch (= 1 tr). * 3 ch, miss 2 sts, 1 tr. Rep from * to end. Finish with 3 ch, miss 2 sts, 1 ss in top of 3 ch.

Row 5: As row 2. Break off.

Three-Colour Motif

3″ (7·5 cm) diameter.

Colour 1:

5 ch in a ring.

Row 1: 6 ch (= 1 tr, 3 ch) * 1 tr, 3 ch. Rep from * to make 6 ch sps. Break off. Join on colour 2 at any tr.

Row 2: 1 dc into tr, 5 tr in ch sp. Rep. Break off. Join on colour 3 at any dc.

Row 3: 4 ch, 1 dc in dc of previous row. Rep.

Row 4: 4 ch, 5 dtr, 4 ch in ch sp, 1 dc in dc of previous row. Rep. Break off.

Five-point golden star

Scandinavians have a charming custom at Christmas when they hang a golden star in a window, sometimes made of straw, sometimes in crochet or even in gold paper.

This is generally lit by the four Advent candles which again are to be seen in the window of every house or flat at that time. We can always learn from the customs of other countries, so here is a golden star, in crochet.

You will need

1 ball Goldfingering (which will make two stars)

1 lampshade ring 8″ (20·3 cm)

Hook No. 3·5 or 3·0

Method

4 ch in a ring.

1 1 tr, 2 ch eight times. Ss to first tr (i.e. 3 ch).

2 3 dc in each ch sp (24 dc).

3 Dc, inc in every 4th st (30 dc).

4 Dc without increasing.

5 Dc, inc every 6th st (35 dc).

6 Dc, inc every 7th st (40 dc).

7 3 ch (= 1 tr) 5 ch * miss 3 dc, 1 tr, 5 ch. Rep (10 sps). Ss into first tr then into ch sp.

8 3 ch, 6 tr in first ch sp, 1 tr into tr, 7 tr in next ch sp, 3 ch (= 15 tr). Rep to end. Join to top of 3 ch.

9 Ss to 2nd tr. * 13 tr, 7 ch, rep, missing first tr of each tr gr. Join.

10 Ss to 2nd tr. * 11 tr, 5 ch, ss over 7 ch sp, 5 ch. Rep, missing first tr. Join.

11 Ss to 2nd tr. * 9 tr, 13 ch. Rep.

12 Ss to 2nd tr. 7 tr, 9 ch, ss over 13 ch sp, 9 ch. Rep.

13 Ss to 2nd tr. * 5 tr, 6 ch, ss over 9 ch sp, 9 ch, ss over 2nd loop, 6 ch. Rep.

14 Ss to 2nd tr. * 3 tr, 4 ch, ss over loop (9 ch, ss over next loop, twice), 4 ch. Rep.

15 Ss to 2nd tr. * 1 tr into 2nd and 3rd trs (9 ch, ss over loop, three times). Rep. Don't break off.

Using sewing cotton, oversew crochet to ring attaching points of star firmly and catching up the chain loops in the centre of each. Now using hook, work dc closely round ring working over crochet at these points. Join after working all round and make a 9″ (22·8 cm) ch, or required length. Take out sewing cotton.

Simple open star

While the golden star is kept for Christmas, window and wall hangings made in the same way but in white or colours, are popular all the year round. Here are three designs for window decorations, the first very simple and easily made, the two following slightly more complicated but very pretty. The crochet motif when finished must be stretched tightly into the ring and should be at least 1½″ (3·75 cm) smaller in diameter than the size of the ring.

You will need

1 ball Crysette, any similar cotton or lurex mixture yarn, e.g. Starspun.

Hook No. 3 or appropriate size.

Metal ring, preferably white-coated, 8″ (20 cm) in diameter (lampshade rings, sold at needlework shops and large stores)

Method

Make 15 ch in a ring.

1 36 tr (3 ch at beginning = 1 tr).

2 (Work this and successive rows into back loop of trs only) 12 grs of 3 tr with 2 ch between.

3–6 Grs of 3 trs as in row 2, but inc 1 ch between grs in every row. Row 6, therefore has 6 ch between grs.

7 3 tr, 10 ch. Rep.

8 1 dc in middle of 3 tr gr. In the ch sp work 1 dc, 1 htr, 6 tr, 3 ch, 6 tr, 1 htr, 1 dc. Rep. Don't break off.

Stretch into ring, attaching with strong sewing cotton at every 3 ch point.

Then dc all round ring firmly—about 24 dc between each point. Leave an end for hanging. Take out sewing cotton if visible.

Lacy window decoration

You will need

1 ball Lysbet, or similar
Hook No 2·50 or appropriate
Metal ring, 7″ or 18 cm diameter

Method

Make ring of 10 ch.

Row 1:   35 dc.

Row 2:   * 4 dc, inc 1. Rep.

Row 3:   Miss 2 sts. * (3 tr, 3 ch, 3 tr) in next, miss 2 sts,
1 dc. Rep from *. Join with ss (7 points).

Row 4:   1 ss in next 3 sts. * (1 dc, 3 ch, 1 dc) in ch sp,
10 ch. Rep from *. Join with ss.

Row 5:   * (1 dc, 3 ch, 1 dc) in 3 ch, 6 ch (1 dc, 3 ch, 1 dc)
round 10 ch, 6 ch. Rep from *. End with ss in first dc.

Row 6:   1 ss into 3 ch sp, 3 ch, 2 tr, 3 ch, 3 tr in same ch
sp. * 1 dc round 6 ch sp (3 tr, 3 ch, 3 tr) in next 3 ch sp
* 1 dc round 6 ch sp (3 tr, 3 ch, 3 tr) in next 3 ch sp.
Rep from *. End with ss.

Row 7:   ss to 3 ch sp. * 1 dc in ch sp, 10 ch. Rep.

Row 8:   1 ss in 5 following ch, 1 dc in same ch sp * 12 ch,
1 dc in following 10 ch sp. Rep from *.

For a larger star, rows 5 and 6, 7 and 8 may be repeated.
Star must be stretched tightly into ring, sewn,
then dc all round.

Large white star

You will need

I ball cotton, e.g. Stalite or Crysette, or 3-ply yarn,
wool or lurex mixture
No 3·50 hook, or suitable
Metal ring about 8″ (20 cm) in diameter

Method

Work 8 ch into ring.

Row 1:   3 ch (= 1 tr) 23 tr (= 24 tr).

Row 2:   5 ch (= 1 tr and 2 ch) * miss 1 tr, 1 tr in next tr,
2 ch Rep. Join with ss to 3rd ch.

Row 3:   4 ch (= 1 dtr). 1 dtr, 4 ch, 2 dtr round first sp,
* 2 dtr, 4 ch, 2 dtr in next sp. Rep from *. Join to ch.

Row 4:   7 tr in each sp, 1 dc between grs of 4 dtr.

Row 5:   1 ss in next 4 sts, 11 ch (= 1 tr and 8 ch) * miss
3 tr, 1 dc, 3 tr, 1 tr in next tr, 8 ch. Rep from * and join
to 3rd ch with ss.

Row 6:   5 ch (= 1 tr and 2 ch) * miss 2 ch, 1 tr in next ch,
2 ch. Rep from * (36 tr).

Row 7:   4 ch (= 1 dtr) 1 dtr, 4 ch, 2 dtr in first sp. * miss 1 sp,
2 dtr, 4 ch, 2 dtr in next sp. Rep from *.

Row 8:   4 tr, 1 dtr, 4 tr round every ch sp, 1 dc between
grs of dtr.

Row 9 if necessary: ss to dtr, then * 5 ch, ss to dtr making
a picot, 8 ch join to next dtr. Rep.

Star should fit tightly to ring. Attach each picot then dc all
round ring with hook, covering ring completely.
Leave end for hanging up.

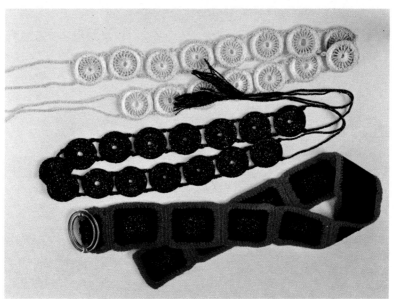

1 Top and middle : two versions of a ring belt (see page 37)
  Bottom : square motif belt (see page 53)

2 Shoulder bag (see page 56)

3 Shawl with square motifs (see page 50)

⑩Black wall hanging

Hanging on a white wall, this has the appearance of fine wrought iron-work especially when made in black 'Goldfingering'.

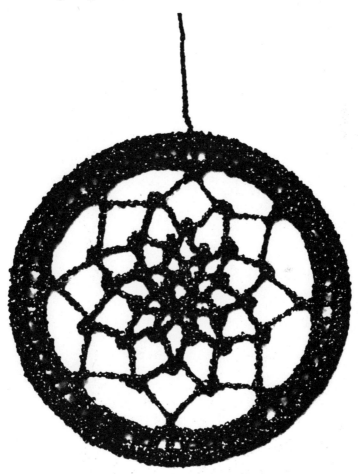

You will need

½ oz Lurex mixture, cotton, yarn, or Twilley's Goldfingering
Hook No 3·00 or appropriate
Metal ring 7″ (18 cm) in diameter

Method

Make 7 ch into a ring.

Row 1:   16 dc.

Row 2:   1 dc, 5 ch, miss 1 dc. Rep. Break off.

Row 3:   Start in middle ch of a loop. * 1 dc, 3 ch, 1 dc
(making 1 picot) in ch. 7 ch. Rep from *. Join to first dc.
Break off.

Row 4:   Row 3 with 9 ch between.

Row 5:   Row 3 with 11 ch between.

Row 6:   * 1 dc in middle ch of loop 13 ch. Rep from *.

Row 7:   1 dc on dc, 13 dcs over chs (112 dc).

Row 8:   4 ch. * miss 1 dc, 1 tr into next dc, 1 ch. Rep from *.
Join to third ch of first 4 ch.

Press, shape and if necessary make another row dc all round,
otherwise sew to ring. (Shape must be **stretched** into ring.)
Dc all round, working through trs and with 3 dc between
each.

Leave end for hanging. This may be made into a chain,
though a single thread is quite strong enough for this purpose.

Blue Lurex
wall decoration

(or colour of choice)

You will need

1 metal ring, 6″ (15 cm) in diameter
½ oz Lurex mixture, yarn or cotton
Hook No 3·00 or suitable

Method

Make 8 ch into a ring.

Row 1:   3 ch (= 1 tr) 23 tr, join to top ch.

Row 2:   6 ch (= 1 dtr + 2 ch) * miss 1 sp, 1 dtr, 2 ch in
next sp. Rep from *, join to 4th ch.

Row 3:   1 dc on each dtr, 3 dc over each 2 ch of previous
row (48 dc).

Row 4:   4 ch (= 1 dtr) 1 dtr in same sp, 5 ch * 2 dtr in
next sp, miss 2 sps, 2 dtr in next sp, 5 ch. Rep from *,
ending with 2 dtr (12 points).

Row 5:   4 tr, 3 ch, 4 tr over each ch sp, 1 dc between grs
of dtrs.

Row 6:   Ss over 4 tr and 1 ch. * 1 dc in second ch, 9 ch.
Rep from * all round.

Star must be stretched into ring and row 6 may be omitted
altogether. If star is too small, more chain may be made
between each point in row 6 in order to achieve size.
Sew into ring, then dc all round. Leave end for hanging up.

A ring belt

You will need

15 rings, diameter 1½″ (4 cm) for a belt measuring
1 yard (90 cm)
1 ball Lurex 'Starspun', or choice
Hook No 2·50

Method

1st ring:

5 ch in a ring. 4 ch, 20 dtr. Join with ss.

1 dc over metal ring, then working over ring throughout
* 3 dc in each of the first 5 dtrs, 5 ch (loop), ss to top of
previous dc. Rep from * to end. Join with ss, break off.

2nd and succeeding rings:

Work as before until two loops completed. 3 dc in each of
the next 5 sts, 2 ch, 1 ss in a 5 ch loop of the first ring,
2 ch, ss to previous dc, 3 dc in each of the next 5 sts, 2 ch,
ss to second loop of first ring, 2 ch, ss to previous dc,
3 dc in each of the next sts. Join with ss. Break off.

Continue until all rings are covered and joined together.

(See colour plates.)

CORDS FOR TYING

Cut twelve lengths yarn about 33″ (85 cm). Take three of

these and thread through a 5 ch loop at end of belt.
Plait them until 4″ (10 cm) remain, knot leaving tassel.

Make similar plaits on three remaining loops.

Three medallions

Very small amounts of Lurex yarn and 'Goldfingering' can be used for these attractive pendants—'jewellery' favoured by the young!

White medallion

Using white and silver yarn, hook No 2 or 2·5, ring 1¼″ (3 cm) diameter, 4 ch in a ring. 2 ch, 20 tr, join. Working over ring, 3 dc in each tr. Join.

A small pearl may be stuck in the centre with adhesive.
Make a chain about 1 yard (90 cm) of silver thread if
available or of the same yarn as pendant.

Gold medallion

Using gold 'Goldfingering', ring $1\frac{3}{4}''$ ($4\frac{1}{2}$ cm) diameter,
hook 2·5, 4 ch in a ring, 1 ch, 12 dc. Join. * Yoh, insert
hook into first st, draw through a loop, rep once, yoh,
draw through all loops, 3 ch. Rep from *.

Working over ring * 2 dc in 3 ch sp, 2 dc over ring.
Rep from *. Join, don't break off.

Finish with loop for neck chain, making length required.

Black medallion

Using black 'Goldfingering' or black Lurex mixture,
hook No 2·5, ring 2'' (5 cm), 5 ch in a ring.

Row 1: 1 ch, 16 dc. Join to 1 ch.

Row 2: 2 ch * yoh, insert hook in same st, draw through a
loop stretching slightly. Rep twice from *. Yoh, draw through
all loops, 1 ch. Rep making 16 puff sts. Join.

Row 3: Working over ring, make 2 dc in top of puff st
and 3 dc in the 1 ch between. Join, then make neck chain
required length. Join.

Table mat with rings

Instructions are given for one mat as shown. This can be
used as a centre piece or for any other purpose where a round
mat is required. A luncheon or dinner-table set could be
made with six or eight of them, when any of the thicker
crochet cottons, in chosen colour could be used, or like the
original, made in Jaeger 'Summer Spun' which is available
in natural and pastel shades.

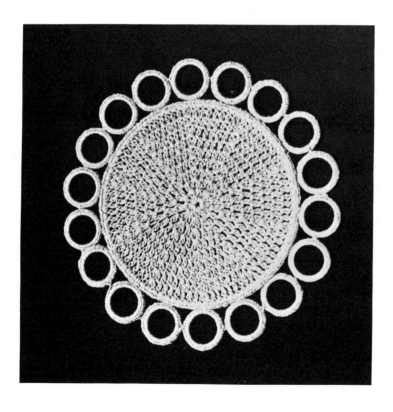

You will need

2 balls 'Summer Spun'
Hook No 3·00
1 white lampshade ring, 8″ (20 cm) in diameter
18 rings, 2″ (5 cm) in diameter

Method

Group treble stitch is used for centre of mat (gtr). See p. 15 for stitch. Each row begins with 3 ch and ends with ss into the top of the 3 ch. After the first row of gtrs which is worked over the chain ring, all following rows are worked *between* stitches.

Make 5 ch, join in a ring.

Row 1:   Make 10 gtr over ring. Join.

Row 2:   Inc 1 st in every sp (20 sts).

Row 3:   Inc 1 st in every other sp (30 sts).

Row 4:   Inc 1 st in every 3rd sp (40 sts).

Row 5:   Inc 1 st in every 4th sp (50 sts).

Row 6:   Inc 1 st in every 5th sp (60 sts).

Row 7:   Inc 1 st in every 6th sp (70 sts).

Row 8:   Inc 1 st in every 7th sp (80 sts).

Row 9:   Inc 1 st in every 8th sp (90 sts).

The motif should now be about 1″ (2·5 cm) less in diameter than the large ring (it must be stretched into the ring). If too small, owing to the use of different cotton, add a further row, if too large, take out one row.

Now working over ring, make 3 dc between every st, attaching motif to ring.

Join with ss.

Cover smaller rings in pairs, as follows: work dc over one ring until tight and firm, about 50 sts. Join with ss then without breaking off continue over second ring. Join with ss and break off. Join pairs of rings into a circle and attach evenly to large ring, sewing with Sylko.

Smaller mats can be made similarly with one ring $4\frac{1}{2}''$ (11 cm) in diameter and twelve rings $1\frac{1}{2}''$ (4 cm) in diameter.

Edwardian centre mat

The 'table centre' is not now often used, but this old design
is too pretty to be neglected. The example shown is worked
in black 'Goldfingering' and would make an occasional mat
or a wall hanging if encased in a metal ring as described on
previous pages. But most attractive would be a luncheon
set made in one of the colours of this same yarn, or in any
other. It measures 8½" (21 cm) in diameter, and could be
made smaller by omitting the last two rows or larger by
adding a shell or lacy edge.

You will need

For one mat as illustrated, use hook No 3·00 and about two-thirds of a ball of 'Goldfingering'.

Method

Make 8 ch in a ring.

1   3 ch, 23 tr.

2   6 ch (= 1 tr, 3 ch). * miss 1 tr, 1 tr, 3 ch. Rep from * all round (12 ch sps).

3   Tr in each tr, 5 tr in ch sps.

4   * 5 tr in first tr, 3 ch, miss 5 tr. Rep all round. (Groups of trebles are in line with trebles in round 2.)

5   This, in effect, is two rounds worked at the same time. * Work 1 tr into each of the 5 tr of previous round, but leave last st of each on hook then draw through altogether making a group. 5 ch, 4 dtr worked into the top of this group, again leaving the last st of each on the hook, drawing through all to form a leaf cluster. 5 ch, 4 dtr worked into the top of *this* leaf cluster, making another. Rep from * all round, joining to top of first 5 tr group. Break off.

6   Starting at top join of two leaf clusters, make 1 dc, 11 ch. Rep.

7   1 tr on dc, 15 trs over ch. Rep.

8   1 tr, 3 ch, miss 3 tr. Rep.

9   Tr on tr, 4 tr over 3 ch. Rep. Break off, unless further pattern or edging is added to increase size.

Large round floor mat

A mat with several possibilities, depending on thickness of yarn used. Can be made in dish-cloth cotton, used double, for a strong washable mat for a bathroom floor. Using a finer cotton, it makes an attractive cover for a round table. Worked in string, though hard on the hands, it makes a tough useful mat for a porch or doorway—looks good, too, on a wooden or tiled floor.

You will need

For table mat: 2 hanks Twilley's S 17 Cotton, white.
Hook No 4·50

For bathroom mat: 4 four-ounce hanks thick dish-cloth cotton.
Hook No 5·00

For floor mat: 1 lb Garden Twine, 3-ply jute or similar, or any of the strong synthetic yarns which are available.
Hook No 5·00

Method

10 ch in a ring.

1   3 ch (= 1 tr) 19 tr. Join.

2   3 ch * 3 ch, miss 1 tr, 1 tr. Rep. End with 3 ch, 1 ss in top of first 3 ch.

3   Ss into ch sp. 3 ch, 2 tr in ch sp. * 2 ch, 3 tr in ch sp. Rep. End with 2 ch, ss in top of 3 ch.

4   3 ch, 1 tr in same st, 1 tr in next tr, 2 tr in next tr. * 2 ch, 2 tr in 1 tr, 1 tr, 2 tr in last tr of gr. Rep.

5   3 ch, 1 tr in same st, 3 tr, 2 tr in last tr, 2 ch. Rep (blocks of 7 tr, 2 ch).

6   As row 5, but with blocks of 9 tr, 2 ch.

7   1 tr in every tr, 1 tr in ch sp.

8   3 ch (= 1 tr) * 2 ch, miss 1 tr, 1 tr. Rep.

9   Ss into ch sp. 3 ch, 2 tr in same ch sp. * 3 tr in each ch sp. Rep.

10   3 ch, 6 tr. * 2 ch, miss 1 tr, 14 tr. Rep. End with 2 ch, 7 tr, 1 ss in top of 3 ch.

11   3 ch, 4 tr. * 2 ch, miss 1 tr, 1 tr in tr, 1 tr in ch sp, 1 tr in tr, 2 ch, miss 1 tr, 10 tr. Rep. End with 2 ch, miss 1 tr, 1 tr in tr, 1 tr in ch sp, 1 tr in tr, 2 ch, miss 1 tr, 5 tr, ss in top of 3 ch.

12   3 ch, 4 tr. * 1 tr in ch sp, 1 tr in tr, 2 ch, miss 1 tr, 1 tr in tr, 1 tr in ch sp, 10 tr. Rep. End with 1 tr in ch sp, 1 tr in tr, 2 ch, miss 1 tr, 1 tr in tr, 1 tr in ch sp, 5 tr. Ss in top of 3 ch.

13   3 ch. * 1 tr in every tr and 1 tr in ch sps. Rep.

14–19   As rows 8–13.

20   3 ch (= 1 tr). * 3 ch, miss 2 tr, 1 tr. Rep. End with
3 ch, miss 2 tr. Ss.

21   Ss into ch sp. 3 tr in same ch sp. * 4 tr in each ch sp.
Rep.

22   3 ch, 2 tr, * 1 picot (6 ch, 1 ss in first ch), miss 1 tr,
3 tr. Rep.

OR

Last row may be omitted and fringe substituted, as in
illustration. Make a final row of 1 dc, 3 ch, miss 2 tr, rep.
Then cut lengths of cotton 7″ (17·5 cm). Using three lengths
together, knot a tassel in each chain space.

OR

Further rows may be added, as in illustration, or even more,
by repeating pattern.

4   Joseph's coat (see page 65)

5 Jerkin (see page 59)

6 Two versions of a one-motif cushion (see page 54)

SQUARES

Shawl with square motifs

A shawl is perhaps the one garment which can be worn all
one's life, from early infancy to old age. Never unfashionable,
always a comfort, its colour and design become more
sophisticated as one gets older, though eventually one might
revert to the white innocence of a baby shawl again towards
the end of one's days.

This can be made in any colour scheme, to suit any age and
occasion. The original was in four shades of blue including
angora which gives luxury and interest. Both Lurex yarn
and mohair might be used in motifs for an evening shawl—
very useful in black. (See colour plates.) And, of course,
any square motif can be used (see illustration below).

You will need

8 ozs 4-ply wool, main colour (mc)
1 oz each two other shades (dark col 1, light col 2)
2 ozs mohair or six ½ oz balls angora
Hooks No 3·5 and 4·5

Method

Motifs are approx. 4″ (10 cm) square. Use 3·5 hook

1 Mc. Make 4 ch, join in a ring. 1 dc, 3 ch four times.
Ss to first dc.

2 Ss to first 3 ch sp. 3 ch (= 1 tr), 2 tr, 2 ch, 3 tr into sp
(3 tr, 2 ch, 3 tr) 3 times. Ss into third ch, break off.

3 Col 1. Join to a 2 ch sp, 1 dc in sp, 3 ch, 1 dc in same sp,
3 ch, 1 dc between grs, 3 ch. Rep all round. Ss to first dc.

4 Ss in first 3 ch sp (3 tr, 2 ch, 3 tr) in corner, 3 tr in each
of next two sps. Rep to end. Ss to third ch. Break off.

5 Col 2. Join to a 2 ch sp. * 1 dc in sp, 3 ch, 1 dc in same
sp, 3 ch (1 dc between tr gr, 3 ch) three times. Rep from *
to end. Ss to first dc.

6 As 4th, but working 3 tr into each of 4 sps between grs.
Break off.

7 With mohair or angora and 4·5 hook, work 1 tr into every
other tr, 4 tr in corner.

Make 20 motifs. Sew together with wool matching last row,
into 'v' shape as shown in diagram. Now with mc, start at
corner indicated and work lattice st—1 tr, 1 ch—all round.
At inner 'v' dec (2 trs together) and at outer corners inc,
2 tr, 2 ch, 2 tr in corner st. Work 8 rows thus, then 1 further
row on outside edges. If liked, more rows may be worked
on outer edges to make a wider shawl.

Diagram for shawl with square motifs

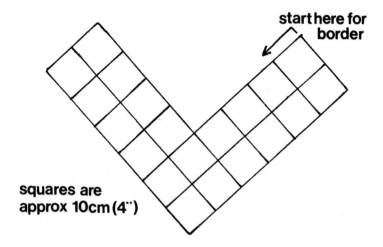

start here for border

squares are approx 10cm (4")

For fringe, cut lengths of mc 16″ (40 cm) and make a tassel in every other lattice on outside edges.

Motif belt

The same motif, or indeed any other square one, can be
converted into a belt. Again the mixing of colours and yarns
gives interest. The original was in chocolate and gold
lurex mixture (centre), dark brown 4-ply wool, outlined
with flame-coloured mohair and wool mixture. This makes
an attractive finish to a dark brown jersey and skirt or dress.

(See colour plates.)

For a belt measuring 37″ (94 cm) make 11 motifs (omitting
row 7) about 3″ (7·6 cm) square in own choice of materials.
Join together. Press length of adhesive binding on wrong
side, stretching motifs to make them rectangular.
(Woolworth's carpet binding was used.)

Finish with clasp or buckle.

One-motif cushion

A little 'scatter' cushion, both sides alike, taking only two ounces of 4-ply wool. Other medium may be used. Cushion pad can be in self or contrasting colour.

You will need

2 ozs 4-ply wool or choice of material
Hooks No 4·00 and 3·50

Method

With hook No 4·00 7 ch in a ring.

Row 1:   4 ch, 4 dtr, 5 ch (5 dtr, 5 ch) 3 times. Join to top of 4 ch. Ss across top of 4 dtr, 1 ss in next ch sp.

Row 2:   3 ch, 2 tr, 3 ch, 3 tr in ch sp. * 4 ch, 3 tr, 3 ch, 3 tr in ch sp. Rep from * end with 4 ch. Ss to top of 3 ch.

Row 3:   3 ch, 1 tr in each of next 2 trs, * 3 tr, 3 ch, 3 tr in ch sp, 1 tr in each of next 3 trs, 1 ss in ch sp, 3 ch, 1 tr in each of next 3 trs. Rep from *. End with ss in 3 ch.

Row 4:   3 ch, 5 tr. * 3 tr, 3 ch, 3 tr in ch sp, 6 tr, 4 ch, 6 tr. Rep from *. Join with ss.

Row 5:   3 ch, 8 tr, * 3 tr, 3 ch, 3 tr in ch sp, 9 tr (3 ch, 1 ss, 3 ch) in 4 ch sp, 9 tr. Rep.

Row 6:   3 ch, 11 tr. * 3 tr, 3 ch, 3 tr in corner, 12 tr, 4 ch, 12 tr. Rep.

Row 7:   8 ch, miss 5 tr, 1 tr in each of next 9 tr. * 3 tr, 3 ch, 3 tr in corner, 9 tr, 5 ch, miss 5 tr, 9 tr. Rep.

Row 8:   6 ch, 1 ss in ch sp, 3 ch, 1 tr in next tr, 5 ch,
miss 5 tr, 1 tr in each of next 6 trs. * 3 tr, 3 ch, 3 tr in
corner, 6 tr, 5 ch, miss 5 tr, 1 tr (3 ch, 1 ss, 3 ch) 1 tr, 5 ch,
1 tr (3 ch, 1 ss, 3 ch) 1 tr, 5 ch, miss 5 tr, 6 tr. Rep from *.

Row 9:   8 ch, 1 tr in next tr (3 ch, 1 ss, 3 ch), 1 tr in next tr,
5 ch, miss 5 tr, 3 tr. * 3 tr, 3 ch, 3 tr in corner, 3 tr, 5 ch,
miss 5 tr, 1 tr (3 ch, 1 ss, 3 ch), 1 tr in next tr, 5 ch, 1 tr
(3 ch, 1 ss, 3 ch), 1 tr. Rep from *. Join.

Row 10:   6 ch, 1 ss, 3 ch, 1 tr. Rep lattice pattern to corner.
3 tr, 3 ch, 3 tr in corner. Rep to end.

Row 11: 8 ch, 1 tr, 4 tr in ch sp, 1 tr in tr, 5 ch, 1 tr in tr,
4 tr in ch sp, 3 tr in next 3 tr, 3 tr, 3 ch, 3 tr in corner,
3 tr, 4 tr in ch sp, 1 tr in tr. Rep pattern to end.

Row 12:   4 tr in each ch sp, trs in each tr, corners as
before. Break off.

Make a second side similarly, then without breaking off,
join the two sides together, working through both edges:
4 dc, 1 picot. Rep. Work round 3 sides leaving wool to
complete 4th side after inserting filled pad. Use hook 3·50
for edges. Make this 11½″ (29 cm) square.

Shoulder bag

Little flowers embedded in a mohair surround make a very pretty bag which a child would appreciate—or her mother. The original was in blues and white but any colour scheme and variety of wools would be attractive. (See colour plates.) Motif panel, back and front, measures 9″ (22·5 cm).

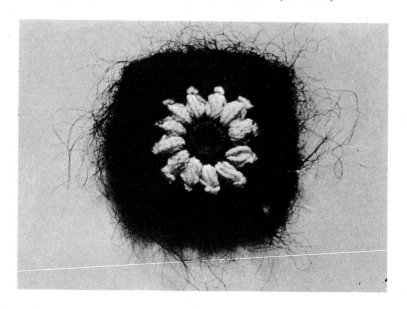

You will need

1 ball Jaeger mohair
About ½ oz white crêpe 4-ply wool
1 oz Jaeger 'Gaelic Spun' saxe blue
½ oz dark blue double knitting
Hooks No 3·50 and 4·00
(Obviously oddments of various wools could be used)
Buckram, or other stiffening, lining and a 7″ (17·5 cm) zip

Method

FLOWER MOTIF
(See opposite)

Make 5 ch in a ring, using saxe blue and 3·50 hook.

Row 1:   12 dc, join, break off. Join on white.

PUFF STITCH

Yoh, hook into stitch, draw through a loop. Rep twice.
Yoh, draw through all loops, 1 ch to complete.

Row 2:   Work between dcs, 12 puff sts with 1 ch between each. Join, break off.

Row 3:   With dark blue, join at a ch sp. 2 tr in each of 3 sps, 2 ch (corner). Rep all round. Join, break off.

Row 4:   With mohair, dc in every st, 3 dcs at corners.

Row 5:   Dc in every st, 2 dcs in corner st. Break off, leaving short end for sewing.

Make 18.

SIDE BAND

Using saxe blue and No 4·00 hook make 10 ch.
Work 9 dc on 144 rows.

SHOULDER STRAP

Using saxe blue and No 4·00 hook make 8 ch.
Work 7 dc on 166 rows, tapering to a point at one end (dec 1 st at each end of every row).

TASSEL

Using all wools, cut lengths 10″ (25·5 cm), double them and bind round near the top to make an important tassel.

Sew motifs together with mohair ends making two panels
of nine motifs.

Press lightly then cut shape of panel for lining and stiffening.

Sew side band to panels easing at lower corners.

On inside of opening and using dark blue wool, pick up sts
below the two rows of mohair and work 4 rows dc at each
side of opening. (Zip will be sewn to these two edges.)

Turn inside out, lay on stiffening and sew to the panels,
trimming it slightly smaller. Make up lining with side band
and panels, put on a pocket—which is useful. Sew zip firmly
into opening, hem lining over it and catch to bottom of bag.
A small ring, covered with dc and attached to zip lever
helps to open and close zip more easily.

Sew strap to one side of bag, attach tassel to tapered point
and sew to other side.

The making-up of a handbag is much more laborious than
making the crochet pieces, but time is well spent in
producing a shapely and long-lasting bag!

Jerkin

This is based entirely on the four bright motifs making a panel on each side front. The original was made in black, motifs in shades of pink to purple, and as the main stitch is lattice and fairly elastic will fit figures from 34″–38″. Can be enlarged by adding further rows of lattice stitch to centre fronts. (See colour plates.)

You will need

8 ozs D.K. in black, main colour (mc)
1 oz each of two shades purple (dark, col 1; light, col 2)
Small amount bright pink for motif centres (col 3)
Hook No 4·50

Method

MOTIF
(See previous page)

Row 1:   In col 3, 5 ch in a ring. 16 tr. Break off.

Row 2:   In col 1, 16 tr with 1 ch between each. Break off.

Row 3:   In col 2, join at a ch sp. * 3 tr in each of 3 ch sps,
6 ch, miss 1 ch sp. Rep all round.

Row 4:   In col 1, start at the 2nd tr of the first three tr
block. * 1 tr, 1 ch in every other tr, 7 tr in corner ch sp,
1 ch, miss 1 tr. Rep.

Row 5:   In mc, work dc all round, 3 dc in each corner.
Leave end for sewing. Make 8. Join into two panels of four.

CENTRE FRONTS

Starting at the bottom of panel make lattice st (1 tr, 1 ch,
miss 1) on 40 sts (= 20 trs) for 3 rows. Rep on 2nd panel.

ARMHOLE SHAPING

Starting half-way down 2nd motif from top, work lattice to
bottom of panel (24 trs), turn and work back. * Turn,
dec 1 lattice, work to bottom and back. Rep until you
have 20 trs. Work 4 rows without shaping. Now inc at the
top of every row for back of armhole until there are 23 trs.
Add 28 ch.

ACROSS BACK

Work 8 rows for shoulder (width of motif) then break off.
Start at 3rd tr from top. Work 10 rows straight. Add 6 ch
and work 2nd shoulder, 8 rows. Break off.

Diagram for jerkin

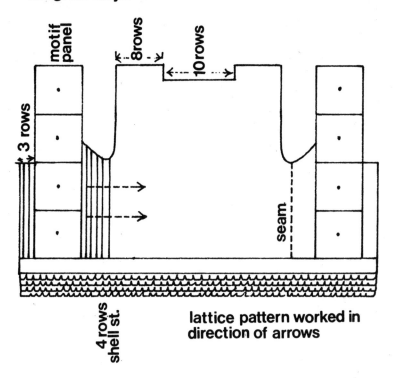

motif panel

8 rows

10 rows

3 rows

seam

4 rows shell st.

lattice pattern worked in direction of arrows

SECOND ARMHOLE

Follow instructions for first, *in reverse* and work as far as '4 rows without shaping'. Work 2 of these and break off. In order that the fronts should look alike, there is a side seam here. Starting on second panel, work as given for 'Armhole Shaping' as far as '4 rows without shaping', work 2 of these then join up side seam.

FINISHING LOWER EDGE

Work 3 rows dc across lower edge then four rows (or more) of shell pattern (though any scalloped pattern may be used).

SHELL PATTERN

Row 1:   3 tr into first st. * miss 2 sts, 1 dc into next st,
miss 2 sts, 5 tr into next. Rep. At end, miss 2 sts, 1 dc into
next, 3 ch turn.

Row 2:   3 tr into first dc. * 1 dc into 3rd tr of 5 tr gr,
5 tr into next dc, and 1 dc.

FINISHING ARMHOLES AND FRONTS

Work 1 row dc, then 1 row corded edging round armholes.
Start at the shell st join, work 1 row dc and 1 row corded
edging round entire fronts. Make a chain about 50″ (134 cm).
Slot cross-wise in every fourth lattice to join fronts.

The squared circle

This square is an experiment with texture using three kinds of wool, crinkled, speckled and plain double knitting, one ounce of each, colours toning from bright to dark. It has several possibilities. Two of them will make a cushion; twenty-eight will make a striking divan cover for a modern setting (4 squares by 7) forty will make a handsome rug for a single bed. They could be developed into a wall-hanging, using four in a chequer-board effect, reversing the colour arrangement in two of them.

To make, use hook No 4·50. Start with 1 oz crinkle spun wool (or perhaps a bouclé—texture is important here). Make a *circle* in dc using up all the wool. Flatten lightly with iron and damp cloth.

Now the circle has to be squared. Fold it into four, marking the four points with cotton for the four corners. Halfway between each mark make another, in different cotton to mark the flat sides of square.

Starting at a corner with speckled wool, make 2 tr in each of the 2 corner sts, 1 tr in each of the next 3 sts, then graduate the height of stitches towards 'flat side' of square from trs, htrs, dcs to ss at cotton mark. Increase the height of stitches correspondingly towards the next corner. Repeat all round. The second round is similar, the third round is in dc, by which time the circle will be a square! Continue until wool is used, making, of course, 2 stitches in each of the 2 corner stitches throughout.

Using the third wool, continue in dc until almost used up, leaving enough to work a length of chain about 52″ (130 cm). Sew this on to circle starting from centre as shown in illustration.

If making into a cushion, the final row can be worked in corded edging for a finish.

Joseph's coat

Made in many colours, this is a striking coat to wear with a polo-necked sweater and pants in black or other dark colour. The snowflake motif is unusual and pretty. Oddments of wool can be used—the more colours the better—with a main colour for final border. White was used for motif centres. Emerald green was chosen for border but several shades of green, from bottle to grass green were used for surrounding each motif so as to avoid monotony. (See colour plates.)

Obviously the colour scheme will depend on what you have and what you want but the total effect should be gay and the arrangement of colours haphazard and non-symmetrical.

You will need

Approximate amounts of 4-ply wool:
2 ozs main colour for borders (mc)
1 oz each three shades main colour for surrounding motifs (smc)
2 ozs each of five assorted bright colours (col 1). And/or oddments
1 oz white for centres (col 2)
Hook No 3·5

Measurements

Large motif 4½″ square (11·35 cm)
Smaller motif 3¾″ square (9·5 cm)
Jacket length from shoulder 32″ (81 cm)
Jacket hangs *loosely* from shoulder and fits almost any figure.
Width at bust level is 40″ (101 cm), at hips, 46″ (126·8 cm), can be worn by a slender or mature figure.

E

Method

SNOWFLAKE MOTIF

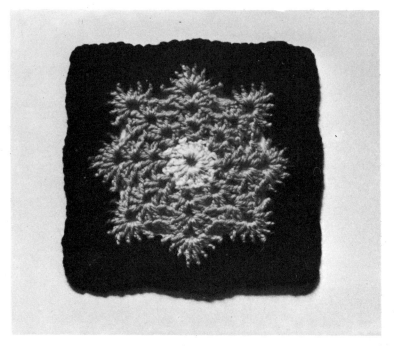

Using col 2, make 6 ch, join in a ring.

Round 1:   3 ch, 15 tr in ring. Join with ss in 3rd ch.
Fasten off. Join col 1 to any tr.

Round 2:   5 ch, 1 tr in same tr * miss 1 tr (1 tr, 2 ch, 1 tr)
in next st. Rep from * 6 times, miss 1 tr, ss in 3rd ch.

Round 3:   Ss into 1st ch sp, 5 ch, 2 tr in same 2 ch sp
(2 tr, 2 ch, 2 tr) in each 2 ch sp to end, 1 tr in same 2 ch sp
as ss. Join with ss in 3rd ch.

Round 4:   Ss into 1st ch sp, 5 ch, 3 tr in same 2 ch sp
(3 tr, 2 ch, 3 tr) in each 2 ch sp to end, 2 tr in same 2 ch sp
as ss. Join with ss in 3rd ch.

Round 5:   Ss into 1st ch sp, 5 ch, 4 tr in same 2 ch sp
(4 tr, 2 ch, 4 tr) in each 2 ch sp to end. 3 tr in same 2 ch sp
as ss. Join with ss to 3rd ch. Fasten off. Join smc with ss
to any 2 ch sp.

Round 6:   (worked in spaces between trs, not into trs).
* 1 dc in next sp, 1 htr in next sp, 1 tr in each of next 5 sps
(2 tr, 3 ch, 2 tr) in 2 ch sp (corner), 1 tr in each of next
5 sps, 1 htr in next sp, 1 dc in next, ss in 2 ch sp. Rep from *
3 times, working last ss in ss at beginning of round.

Round 7:   3 ch. * 1 tr in each st to corner sp (2 tr, 4 ch, 2 tr)
in corner sp. Rep from * 3 times. 1 tr in each st to 3 ch.
Join with ss in 3rd ch. Fasten off.

Make 40 squares. Sew together in four rows of ten.

Make 26 smaller squares, by omitting round 5 and adjusting
the stitches in round 6 to correspond. Sew these together as
shown in three top rows of diagram, i.e. one row of ten
squares, four at fronts and eight across back.

Diagram for Joseph's coat
shoulder shapings

Now join lower to upper part of jacket, easing in larger squares to meet the smaller. Shape shoulders. Starting at armhole edge, work 11 dc, 1 htr, 13 tr. Break off. Rep on each shoulder. Join seams.

Now make 2 rows dc all around outer edges of garment with 4 dc at corners. Work armholes to match. Make cord or thick chain 30″ (76 cm). Slot through spaces at corners of top squares to tie.

Using the smaller motifs and planning to size, this makes an attractive coat for a child.

Cover-up garment for an eight-year-old

It is quicker to make a motif in one colour than in several because the breaking off and joining on of different wools takes up time. Yet delightful effects can be produced from solid-coloured squares or hexagons, each in a different colour and arranged to form a pattern. Here is a useful, easily made square, used in this case for a comfortable garment to wear over T-shirt and jeans or skirt, chequer-board in design, bright and cheerful. Can be adapted quite easily for other sizes by making squares larger or smaller. An idea for grown-ups, too.

You will need

4 ozs 4-ply wool, colour 1

3 ozs 4-ply wool, colour 2 (or a variety of colours may be used)

Hooks No 4·00 and 3·50

Method

MOTIF

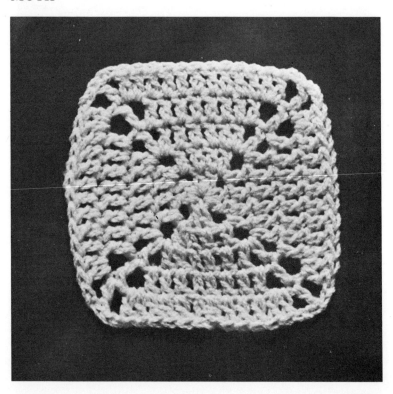

4 ch in a ring using hook No. 4·00.

1   2 ch (= 1 tr) 1 tr, 2 ch. * (2 tr, 2 ch) three times. Join to top of 2 ch.

Diagram for cover-up garment

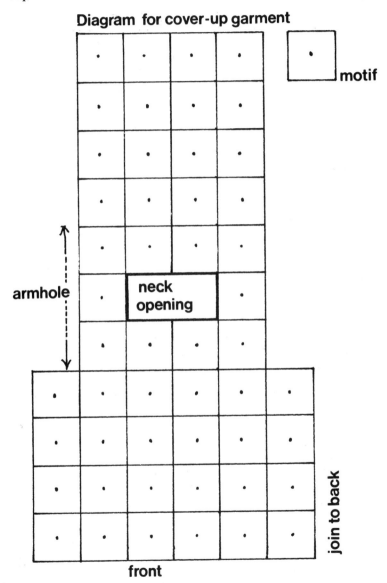

2   2 ch, 1 tr in next tr, (1 tr, 2 ch, 1 tr) in ch sp. * 2 tr,
(1 tr, 2 ch, 1 tr) in ch sp. Rep. Join to top of 2 ch.

3   2 ch, 2 tr. * (1 tr, 2 ch, 1 tr, 2 ch, 1 tr) in ch sp, 4 tr.
Rep. End with 1 tr. Join.

4   2 ch, 3 tr. * (1 tr, 2 ch, 1 tr in tr, 2 ch, 1 tr) in ch sp,
6 tr. Rep. End with 2 tr. Join.

5   2 ch, 4 tr. * (2 tr, 2 ch, 1 tr in tr, 2 ch, 2 tr) in ch sp,
8 tr. Rep. End with 3 tr. Join, break off.

Make 50 motifs, equal numbers of the two colours (or
variegated).

Join together as shown in diagram.

NECK YOKE

Using 3·50 hook and col 1, start at top of shoulder working
dc all round neck.

Decrease at corners (2 sts worked together) and at join of
centre motifs, front and back, work 1 ch across gap to
straighten line. Continue to work for six or seven rows,
decreasing symmetrically at each corner. Finish with 1 row
corded edging.

ARMHOLES

Make similar border round armholes, decreasing at
corners. Finish with corded edge as before.

Slipper from a square

The simplest motif of all!
While instructions are given for an average fitting—
approximately size 5—the pattern can be adjusted easily for
a larger or smaller size.

A paper pattern of the foot is a useful guide, though it is
advisable to make the slipper slightly smaller because the
sole will flatten and stretch with wear.

A useful slipper, comfortable for the elderly, sock-saving for
children to wear indoors, or for anyone.

You will need

3 ozs D.K. wool

Hooks No 4·00 and 4·50

Method

MOTIF

With one strand of wool and hook No. 4·00, make 4 ch and
join in a ring.

1   3 ch, 19 tr.

2   3 ch, 1 tr in same st, 1 tr in each of next 3 trs, 2 tr in next. *
2 ch, 2 tr in next tr, 1 tr in each of next 3 trs, 2 tr in next.
Rep from * twice. 2 ch to end. Join to complete square.

3   3 ch, 6 tr (2 tr, 2 ch, 2 tr) in ch sp. Complete square, 7 tr on each side, (2 tr, 2 ch, 2 tr) in corners, end with (2 tr, 2 ch, 2 tr) join to 3 ch.

4 and 5   As row 3, increasing the number of trs between corners. Break off.

SOLE

Worked with 2 strands of wool, hook No. 4·50.

Make 8 ch and work 2 rows dc on 7 sts. Inc 1 st at each end of next row and work on these 9 sts until there are 18 rows from start. If making a larger sole add further rows here, or for smaller make fewer than 18 rows.

Inc again at each end making 11 sts and work 6 rows. Inc to 13 sts and work 6 rows. Dec at each end of each row until 5 sts remain. Break off.

UPPER

With single wool and 4·00 hook, start at a corner of motif and pick up 10 sts. In dc, work 52 rows or as many as required to stretch round sole. Sew to opposite corner of square, diagonally.

MAKING UP

Pin sole to upper with point of motif to toe and ease in motif so that diagonal points meet the first '13 dc' row of sole. Stretch remainder of upper to remainder of sole. Oversew together on wrong side. Make 1 row dc round upper then 1 row corded edging all round top of slipper to complete.

Finish with flower or tassel trimming.

FLOWER IN TWO COLOURS

Col 1   Hook No. 4·00: 5 ch in a ring. 1 dc, 5 ch, 5 times.

In each chain loop make 1 dc, 4 tr, 1 dc (5 petals). Join and break off.

Col 2   Turn to back of petals already made. Join on to original chain ring between any two dcs. Working at the back, make 1 dc, 7 ch, 5 times, each dc being in between dcs of previous petals. On each of these chain loops make 1 dc, 1 htr, 6 trs, 1 htr, 1 dc. Join and sew to slipper.

OTHER SHAPES

Some of the shapes in this section are very suitable for bedspreads, blankets and rugs. Amounts of cotton or yarn are not included in the instructions because size, tension and materials are so variable. You may want to use some other medium and hook than suggested.

Calculations are easy to do. Make up motifs from one or two balls (or ounces) of chosen material, sew together and measure. If, for example, two balls produce six motifs, then it is possible to assess the number required for the size of bed-cover, cot-cover or whatever you want to make, be it single, double or something in between. Allow also for a simple edging or fringe to finish the outer edge. This could be an extra two ounces for a plain crochet border to a single bedspread, or at least four extra balls of cotton for a fringed double bed-cover.

These hexagonal and octagonal shapes make interesting cushions, too, worked in thick wools and increased in size.

Star-patterned hexagonal for bedspread

Use Crysette, Stalite or any suitable cotton with appropriate sized hook. (See note on amounts of material required, page 77.)

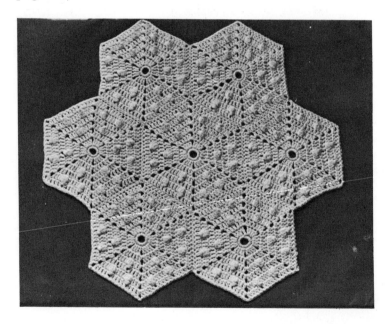

Method

8 ch in a ring.

Row 1:   12 dc in ring. Join with ss.

Row 2:   3 ch (counting as 1 tr), 1 tr, 2 tr in next st, 2 ch,
2 tr in next st, 2 tr in next, 2 ch. Make 6 grs of 4 tr and
2 ch.

Row 3:   3 ch, 1 tr in each of 3 tr, 1 tr, 2 ch, 1 tr in previous
row's ch, 4 tr. Rep to end (6 grs of 6 tr with 2 ch between).

Row 4:   3 ch, 1 bobble. (To make, work 5 tr in the same st,
then take hook out of work, insert it in the top of first tr,
draw loop of last tr through, complete with another
loop through.)

Continue working 4 tr, 2 ch, 3 tr, 1 bobble, 4 tr, 2 ch, end row
with 2 tr and ss into third ch.

Row 5:   3 ch, 6 tr, 2 ch, 10 tr, 2 ch. Rep pattern to end of row.

End with 3 tr and ss into third ch (*miss st at top of each bobble*).

Row 6:   3 ch, 3 tr, 1 bobble, 3 tr, 2 ch, 3 tr, 1 bobble, 3 tr,
2 ch. Rep.

End row with 3 tr, 1 bobble, ss into third ch.

Row 7:   3 ch, 8 tr, 2 ch, 14 tr, 2 ch. Rep. End row with 5 tr and
1 ss.

Motifs are sewn together on wrong side through both loops of
outside edges, making a continuous star pattern.

Starting chains of each row disappear into the pattern!

Little star hexagonal

Very simple, this one, yet most effective when made up.
The sampler opposite was worked in Crysette with hook
No 2·50.

Method

4 ch in a ring. Start each round with 3 ch (= 1st tr).

1 4 grs of 3 trs with 2 ch between.

2 2 tr in 1st tr, 1 tr in next, 2 tr in 3rd tr, 5 ch. Rep. Join to top ch of 3 ch (i.e. 1st tr), in every round.

3 2 tr in 1st tr, 1 tr in each of next 3 trs, 2 tr in last tr, 7 ch. Rep.

4 2 tr in 1st tr, 1 tr in next 5 trs, 2 tr in last, 9 ch. Rep.

Break off, leave end for sewing. Join motifs at treble stitches.

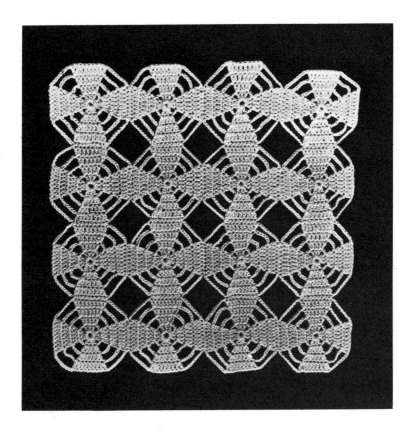

Octagonal with centre square

Flower-like motifs with square to join groups of four, using five colours 4-ply. Hook No 4. Could be made in D.K. with No 5 hook for bold-patterned heavy rug.

Method

N.B.   Start each row at a different chain space.

Col 1, Row 1:   5 ch in a ring. 16 htr. Break off.

Col 2, Row 2:   3 ch in ch sp, then grs of 1 tr, 2 ch, 1 tr in
every other htr. End with 1 tr, 2 ch in 1st ch sp. Join to top of
3 ch. Break off.

Col 3, Row 3:   5 ch, 2 tr in ch sp, then grs of 2 tr, 2 ch, 2 tr
in each ch sp. End with 1 tr in 1st ch sp to complete gr.
Join to 3rd of 5 ch. Break off.

Col 2, Row 4:   5 ch, 3 tr in ch sp. Grs of 3 tr, 2 ch, 3 tr in
each ch sp. End with 2 tr in 1st ch sp to complete. Join to
3rd of 5 ch. Break off.

Col 4, Row 5:   5 ch, 4 tr. Grs of 4 tr, 2 ch, 4 tr in each ch
sp. End with 3 tr in 1st ch sp. Join. Break off.

Col 5, Row 6:   (3 dc in ch sp, 3 htr between 4 tr, 1 tr in gap,
3 htr between 4 tr). Rep. Join.

Col 5, Row 7:   Turn work. Dc in every st on wrong side.

CENTRE SQUARE

In colour 5.

4 ch in a ring.

6 ch, miss 2 sts, 1 dc. Rep (4 loops).

In each loop (2 htr, 2 tr, 2 ch, 2 tr, 2 htr).

Turn work, 1 dc in each st, 2 dc in each corner.

Hexagonal version of circular star

Joined together, this is a suitable motif for a bedspread when any chosen cotton should be used. (See notes on joining up motifs, page 12.)

Method

Start with 15 çh in a ring.

Row 1: 36 tr.

The following rows are worked into the back st of trs.

Row 2: 3 tr, 2 ch (12 grs of 3 tr).

Row 3–5: Inc 1 ch between grs. Row 5 will have 5 ch between trs.

Row 6: 3 tr, 10 ch. Rep.

Row 7: * 1 dc in middle tr of gr (1 dc, 1 htr, 5 tr, 3 ch, 5 tr, 1 htr, 1 dc) in 10 ch sp. Rep.

Row 8: Ss to ch sp (5 ch, 1 tr, 2 ch, 1 tr) in sp. * 10 ch, 1 dc in next ch sp, 10 ch (1 tr, 2 ch, 1 tr, 2 ch, 1 tr) in next ch sp. Rep from * all round. Join with ss to 3rd of 5 ch.

Row 9: 3 ch, 2 tr in ch sp, 2 ch, 2 tr in ch sp, 1 tr on 1 tr. * (1 ch, 1 tr) in alternate ch to next tr gr. (1 tr in 1st tr, 2 tr in 1st ch sp, 2 ch, 2 tr in 2nd ch sp, 1 tr on tr.) Rep from *. Join to 3rd ch.

Row 10: Dc all round.

Anchor motif

In this case, made into a beach bag, but the design could be incorporated into the front of a summer sleeveless jumper or even into a cushion if you have nautical connections! Instructions are given for the beach bag, measuring 36 × 28 cm (14 × 11½″). May be made to any size and in any strong yarn.

Background made in lattice pattern = 1 tr 1 ch. Each dot on chart = 1 tr over 1 ch.

Diagram for anchor

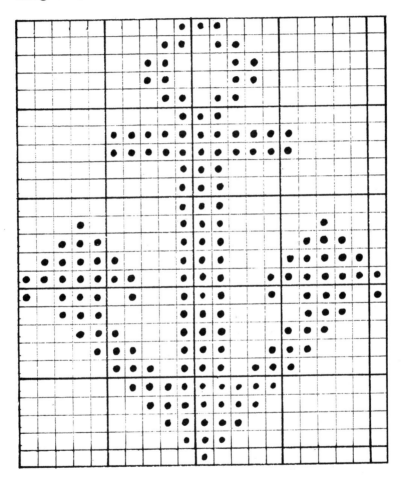

You will need

Approx 4 balls Stalite or similar, hook No 3·50.

Method

Make 67 ch, loosely.

Row 1:   4 ch, 1 tr in 5th ch, 1 ch. * 1 tr, 1 ch, missing 1 ch to the end. Finish with 1 tr.

Continue in lattice patt for 9 rows (tr over tr, ch over ch).

Follow chart for anchor (1 tr in each dotted sp), centralising first dot.

Then 6 rows lattice. Break off.

Pick up stitches across bottom and make 39 rows lattice.

Pin the two sides together. Work 2 dc into each lattice joining front to back, then two further rows dc. Rep on second side.

Work 3 rows dc round top of bag and without breaking off make ch required length for strap loosely, and work 3 rows dc on it. Join to side of bag, finish with tassels or rings.

Line with black Vilene or polythene in dark colour.

ᛰriangular motif

Very pretty in assorted colours for a blanket or rug, or may be made in two colours for pram cover. Illustration shows motifs in pink and white double knitting wool.

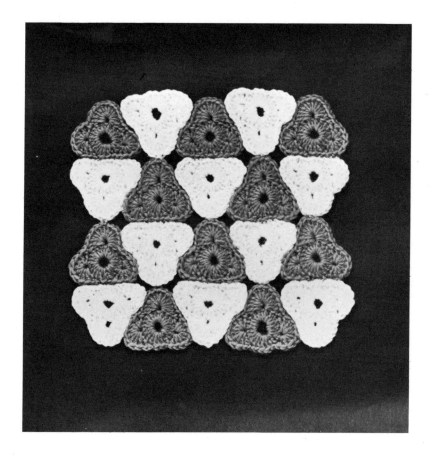

Method

Using hook No. 4·50, 6 ch in a ring. 3 ch, 21 tr over ring. Join.

1 dc in first tr, miss 1 tr, 7 tr in next, miss 2 trs, 1 dc in next tr, miss 2 tr, 12 tr in next tr, miss 2 tr, 1 dc in next, miss 2 tr, 7 tr in next, miss 2 tr, 1 dc. Complete with ss. Break off.

Join together as shown in illustration.

Rectangular table mat

A collection of this kind seems incomplete without the popular
Afghan motif! Though instructions for it were given in the
motif section of *New Ways with Crochet*, it is again included
here in a different shape—a rectangle, as part of the pattern for
a set of luncheon mats.

These are, of course, washable and long wearable, being made
of a finer-than-usual dish-cloth cotton producing a less
bulky but still heat-proof set of mats. Any type of cotton may
be used, however, natural or coloured.

For six mats you will need

4 four-ounce hanks Twilleys S 17 Cotton

Hook No. 4·00.

With thicker cotton a 4·50 hook should be used

Mat measures $11\frac{1}{4} \times 10''$ (28·5 × 25 cms).

Method

Make 12 ch. Work 11 dc for 8 rows. Make 2 dc in the last
st of the eighth row then continue to work *round* the other
3 sides of the rectangle, 5 dcs across short side and 2 dcs
in the last stitch, 9 dcs on long side, 2 dcs in last st, 5 dcs
on short side, join with ss at corner.

Continuing to work round rectangle, 2 ch 2 tr * (= 3 tr) in
first st, 1 ch, miss 1 st, 1 tr in each of next 3 sts, 1 ch, 1 tr
in each of next 3 sts, 1 ch, miss 1 st, 1 ch, 3 tr in last st,
2 ch, 3 tr in first st of short side, 1 ch, miss 1 st, 1 tr in each
of next 3 sts, 1 ch, miss 1 st, 3 tr in last st, 2 ch. Rep from *.
Join to top of 2 ch.

Ss across 2 tr and into first ch sp (*rep at the start of every row*).

Then work in Afghan pattern, 3 tr in each ch sp, 1 ch, and
3 tr, 2 ch, 3 tr in each corner. Join each round with ss into
top of 2 ch. Work 5 rounds. Break off.

Join on again at any corner. Work all round in dc on tr
sts, omitting the 1 ch sps, but with 3 dcs in each corner
ch sp. Join with ss at first corner, turn work and make next
round on wrong side. Continue in dc for 9 rounds working
on alternate sides.

If a bigger mat is required further rounds can be added,
smaller sizes can be made by making fewer rounds of both
stitches.

CROCHET BOOKS PUBLISHED BY MILLS & BOON

Fashion Crochet for Your Doll

Caroline Horne   ISBN 0 263.51480.3

This is a book of instructions for making a completely
modern set of doll's clothes ranging from a smart trouser
suit with peaked cap to a silver mini dress with cape.

210 × 148mm   £1·50 net

112 pages; colour photos; drawings

1st Edition 1970 cased

New Ways With Crochet

Dorothy Standing   . ISBN 0 263.51602.4

This is not a book on how to do crochet but more on how
to use the craft in a modern way. The author puts forward
the interesting and original theory of using paper patterns
and adapting crochet stitches to fit them, thus eliminating
the use of commercial crochet patterns which many people
find difficult to follow.

210 × 148mm   £2·10 net

192 pages; colour plates; drawings

1st Edition 1971 cased

Crochet—Pretty and Practical

Caroline Horne   ISBN 0 263.05151.X

The book is divided into two parts and should contain
something for everyone. There is a selection of pretty
garments (suits, dresses, tabards, jackets, blouses) in the
first part, while the second covers a range of household items
(bedspreads, cushion covers, finger plates, picture tray).

In preparation